Written by
Beth Barber

Editor: Kim Cernek
Illustrator: Darcy Tom
Cover Illustrator: Rick Grayson
Designer/Production: Moonhee Pak/Carrie Rickmond
Cover Designer: Barbara Peterson
Art Director: Tom Cochrane
Project Director: Stephanie Oberc

Table of Contents

Introduction

Effective early childhood educators teach a set of prerequisites for literacy that address how print is organized and presented in books and other printed material. Children who are instructed in these principles, known as concepts of print, are adequately prepared to begin reading in kindergarten or first grade. These concepts are generally taken for granted by an experienced reader, but must be explicitly and repeatedly taught to and practiced by an emergent reader.

Building Blocks for Beginning Readers highlights twelve essential skills emergent readers must master before they can fully participate in a formal reading program. This resource explains each concept and provides tips and fun activities for reinforcing each one.

The initial lessons help children reflect on where they find printed language in their world and how it conveys meaning. Children will also examine how a book is organized and how it is successfully navigated from cover to cover.

The subsequent activities encourage children to actively inspect print. Children will differentiate between uppercase and lowercase letters, examine how letters make words, explore how words make sentences, and identify that a sentence begins with an uppercase letter and ends with punctuation. Children will also learn one-to-one correspondence, left-to-right and top-to-bottom orientation as they practice tracking print. Tips for evaluating children's progress and an assessment tool that incorporates the twelve concepts of print are also included in this resource.

Each section of this book features lessons that show you how to introduce, practice, and reinforce all twelve concepts with children. Each lesson includes a bulleted or bolded list of materials and concise directions for easily incorporating these activities into your regular literacy program.

Building Blocks for Beginning Readers offers teachers and parents simple yet interesting activities that will help the youngest learner acquire the twelve prerequisites for literacy development. It is never too early to begin teaching children the mechanics and concepts that will guide them as print becomes increasingly more important in their lives.

Concepts of Print

In order to become a fluent reader, a child must demonstrate mastery of the following concepts:

1. The reader **recognizes print** in his or her environment.
2. The reader can explain the **purposes of print**.
3. The reader recognizes the front and back **covers** of a book.
4. The reader can identify and define the roles of the book's **author and illustrator**.
5. The reader understands that **print conveys meaning**.
6. The reader differentiates between **uppercase and lowercase letters**.
7. The reader understands that **words are composed of individual letters**.
8. The reader recognizes individual **words**.
9. The reader **differentiates between first and last**.
10. The reader correlates the number of spoken words with the number of printed words on a page, known as **one-to-one correspondence**.
11. The reader understands **directionality**, which includes identifying where to begin reading, tracking text from left to right, turning pages from left to right, and "sweeping" from one line of text to the next.
12. The reader understands that **a sentence begins with an uppercase letter and ends with punctuation**.

These concepts must be explicitly taught through teacher modeling, and children must have repeated opportunities to practice these skills. Use ongoing assessments to track how children are mastering these skills (see pages 47–48).

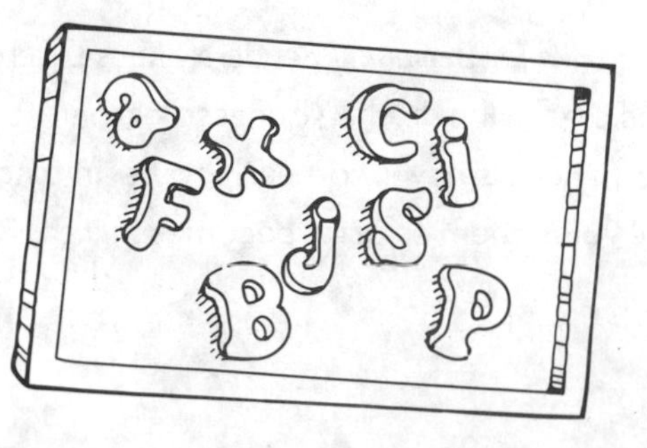

Dear Family,

This is an exciting year for your young learner. He or she will be exploring the skills needed to become a successful reader. Consistent practice at school and at home with the following activities will help your child understand how to become actively involved with printed language:

Focus on print in your environment. Children see print on their toys, clothing, and food packages. Discuss characteristics of the print you discover together.

Discuss with your child why we use printed language. Try involving your child in writing a grocery list or a letter to a friend, pointing out the words *In* and *Out* on the doors to the grocery store, or asking your child to show you the *Exit* sign at his or her favorite restaurant. Highlight for your child other ways you use **printed language in your life**.

When you read with your child, emphasize that a book has **a front cover and a back cover**.

Always read the complete title of a book. Also read the names of the **author and illustrator**, and discuss their roles in preparing the book you are about to read.

Remind children that the words they see in **print mean something**. For example, explain that words might tell a story or record information.

6 Have your child practice differentiating between **lowercase and uppercase letters**.

Review with your child that **words are made up of individual letters**.

Help your child identify **words he or she commonly sees in print**, such as *the* and *we*.

Help your child focus on the **beginning sounds and letters of words**. For example, when you read a book about bears, ask your child to name the first letter of *bear*. When *bear* appears in the text, ask your child to point to the word on the page that begins with *b*.

When sharing a book with your child, **point to each word you read**. This helps your child understand that each word you say corresponds to one word on the page.

Emphasize for your child that when we read, we turn pages from **left to right**. As you use your finger to point to the words you are reading, remind your child that you are reading from left to right, and that when one line ends, you continue with the first word at the left on the next line.

Emphasize for your child that a sentence **begins with an uppercase letter and ends with punctuation**.

All of these skills are taken for granted by an experienced reader. These skills will become natural for your child when he or she experiences them repeatedly.

Sincerely,

Pointers

Copy, color, and cut apart several sets of pictures. Glue each picture to a craft stick to make pointers. Use the pointers in some of the activities in this book.

Recognizing Print

The reader will recognize printed language.

Display greeting cards, books, game boards, trading cards, clothing, food packages, toys, and other items that clearly have print on them. Ask children to name other places they have seen print. Invite children to read any words they can, or ask them to point to and read one of the words on an object.

MATERIALS

- greeting cards
- books
- game boards
- trading cards
- clothing with print
- food packages
- toys

Give each child a Recognizing Print reproducible. Tell children to color the pictures that have print on them.

MATERIALS

- Recognizing Print reproducible (page 9)
- crayons

1 Give children **plastic sunglasses** with the lenses removed, and invite them to "read the room." Encourage children to use their glasses to help them see print in the classroom.

2 Invite children to play a game of I Spy. Identify something in the room that features print, and say *I spy something with print. Listen carefully for your hint.* Describe the object, and encourage children to name it. Play until each child has had an opportunity to name an object.

3 Use **scissors** to cut grocery advertisements from the **newspaper**, and scatter them around the room. Give each child a **paper lunch sack**, and invite children to be "word collectors." Encourage them to collect as many papers with printed words on them as they can find.

4 Collect paper **menus** from local restaurants, and place them at a dramatic play center. Invite children to play "Restaurant," and encourage them to read their menus to each other.

5 Collect small, flat **items with environmental print**—such as paper napkins, trading cards, and cereal box tops—and place them in a large, **cardboard box** at a learning center. Invite children to select examples of print from the box and **glue** them to the side of the box. Encourage children to bring in **examples of print from home** and glue them on the box. Over time, have children identify letters and words they know on the box.

Name ______________________ Date ______________

Recognizing Print

Color the pictures that have words printed on them.

Purposes of Print

The reader will identify the purposes of printed language.

MATERIALS

- map
- recipe book
- empty medicine bottle
- addressed, postmarked envelope
- musical score

Show children a map, and ask them to explain how it is used. Ask children whom they think might use a map (e.g., a bus driver, a cabdriver, a vacationer) and why. Use the same questioning format to investigate who uses a recipe book, a medicine bottle, an envelope, and music—and why. Emphasize for children that all of these items have print on them and that we use this print to help us in our daily lives.

MATERIALS

- Purposes of Print reproducible (page 12)

Give each child a Purposes of Print reproducible. Tell children to draw a line to match each person with the item he or she might read while doing his or her work.

1 Place a **map, recipe book, empty medicine bottle, letter, musical score, paper, pencils,** and **musical instruments** at a dramatic play center. Encourage children to play with these items to explore objects that feature print.

2 Use characters from fairy tales and nursery rhymes in a guessing game. Identify a plot from a story or a rhyme, and use it to pose a question. For example, say *After Goldilocks was chased away by the bears, she sent them a note. What did the bears do when they found the note in their mailbox? What did the note say?* Prompt children to say that the bears read the note that said that Goldilocks was sorry for disrupting their home. Use other scenarios to prompt children to identify purposes of print. For example, say *The prince asked a bird to deliver a message to Rapunzel at the top of the tower. What did Rapunzel do with the message? What did the message say?* or *On Tuesday the bell on the Hickory Dickory Dock clock was broken. How could the mouse tell what time it was when he ran up the clock?*

3 Ask each child's family to write a **letter** to their child and send it to school in a sealed envelope. Inform the families that you will read each child's letter aloud. Place the letters in a **box** with *Mail* written on it. Each day, draw a letter from the box, and ask the class *What should we do with this letter?* Prompt children to respond that you should read it aloud. Read the name on the front of the envelope, and invite that child to stand beside you. Read the letter, and ask children to name reasons why people write letters.

Name ______________________ Date ______________

Purposes of Print

Draw a line to match each person with something he or she might read.

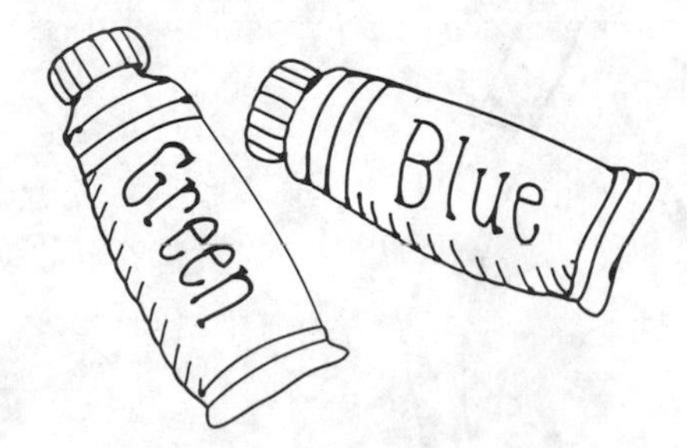

Covers

The reader will identify the front and back covers of a book and demonstrate how to hold a book in the correct reading position.

Invite children to sit in a circle with you. Demonstrate for children how to properly hold a book. Point out the front and back covers of the book, and then read the book to the class. Give each child a book, and encourage children to hold their book in the correct reading position. Ask children if they are looking at the front or back cover. Ask children if the front or back cover is facing the floor.

MATERIALS

- picture books

Tell children they will make book covers. Give each child a piece of construction paper. Invite children to draw a picture on it. On the cover of each child's book, write his or her name in the frame ______*'s Book*. Give each child five pieces of plain paper and another piece of construction paper. Ask children to arrange their papers into a book, and use bookbinding materials to help them bind it. Ask children to identify the front and back covers of their book. Place the books at a learning center, and encourage children to write stories in them.

MATERIALS

- 9" x 12" (23 x 30.5 cm) construction paper
- crayons
- plain paper
- bookbinding materials (e.g., stapler, hole punch/curling ribbon)

1 Set out **five to ten books**, and ask children to stack them in a pile with the front covers facing up.

2 Have children line up books on a **shelf or ledge** with the front covers facing forward and right side up.

3 Invite a child to stand before you, and hand him or her a book with the binding facing the child. Ask the child to pretend to read the book. Determine whether the child positions the book appropriately. Help the child adjust the book if necessary. Repeat the activity with the remaining children.

4 Practice the concepts of front and back by having children take turns standing in front of a **chair**, in back of a chair, at the front of the line, and at the back of the line.

5 Invite children to pretend their body is a book. Tell them their tummy is the front cover and their back is the back cover. Ask children to touch their "front cover" and touch their "back cover."

6 Give each child a book, and play a game. Choose a child. Say *Let's take a look at the **front** cover of **William's** book.* Encourage the child who is named to point to that particular cover of his or her book. (Change the boldfaced words in the sentence prompt to view the front or back covers of another child's book.)

Author and Illustrator

The reader will define the function of the author and illustrator and identify the title of the text.

Display the front cover of a book, and tell children that it has information that helps the reader understand the story. Show children the front covers of various other books, and point out that all of the covers show the title of the book and the names of the author and the illustrator. Tell children that the title is the name of the story and that it sometimes gives the reader clues as to what the story is about. Tell children that the author is the person who thinks of and writes the story. Emphasize for children that thinking about a story is just as important as writing the words. Explain that the illustrator draws the pictures or illustrations for the story. Show children how the title appears across the top of the front cover in large print and how the names of the author and illustrator appear below the title in smaller print. Explain to children that sometimes the author and illustrator are the same person.

MATERIALS

- picture books

Practicing THE Concept

Invite children to be the author and the illustrator of a story. Give each child a piece of paper. Ask each child to dictate a story to you as you write it at the bottom of his or her paper. Ask children to draw an illustration above their dictation. Make a copy of the reproducible for each child. Ask each child to dictate a title for his or her story, and write it on the reproducible. Emphasize that the title should be related to the story. Encourage each child to identify himself or herself as the author and illustrator of the story, and record names in the appropriate places. Invite children to illustrate their cover. Staple a completed reproducible to the front of each child's story.

MATERIALS

- Title/Author/ Illustrated by reproducible (page 17)
- paper
- crayons
- stapler

1 When reading stories together, always read and point to the title of the book, the name of the author, and the name of the illustrator. And ask children the following questions:

What does the author of a story do?
What does the illustrator of a story do?
What is the title of the story?
What does the title help us understand?

2 Invite children to run their finger under the title of the story and point to the names of the author and illustrator whenever you read a book aloud.

3 Over time, children will begin to associate particular characters with their authors and illustrators. Read **books in a series**, such as the "Froggy" books by Jonathan London or Nadine Bernard Westcott's collection of illustrated songs and rhymes. Ask children to name things that are similar in each book in the collection. Show children other books by the same authors and illustrators, but cover their names. Read aloud from a book, and ask children if they can determine the names of the author and illustrator from the style of the words and pictures.

Title ___________________________________

Author ___________________________________

Illustrated by ___________________________

Print Conveys Meaning

The reader will demonstrate comprehension that the print on a page contains meaning.

MATERIALS

- big book
- trade books
- pointer (see page 6)

Display a big book, and open it to the page where the story begins. Use the star pointer to emphasize where to begin reading. Explain to children that the message of the story is in the print or words of the book. Give each child a book and a pointer. Invite children to open their book, and ask them *What do we do if we want to know what happens in a story?* Prompt children to say that we read the words. Say *Point to the place where we find the information in the story.* Prompt children to point to the words on the page. If children point to the illustrations, explain that pictures do help us understand the story, but that the print contains the meaning.

MATERIALS

- Print Conveys Meaning reproducible (page 20)

Give each child a Print Conveys Meaning reproducible. Tell children to look at their paper, and say *You received an invitation in the mail, but I am not sure what it is for. Where can I find this information?* Prompt children to say that you should read the words. Read aloud the text. Ask *How do you find out what the invitation says?* Prompt children to say that you read the text. Ask *Will you go to the party? How will you let Alex know?* Prompt children to say that they could write Alex a note. Invite children to write a note in the space provided. Encourage children to use individual letters or strings of letters to write their message.

1 Encourage children to pretend to read print. This reinforces the concept that print conveys meaning.

2 Encourage children to look through **magazines** and use **scissors** to cut out words. Cut out a large circle from **blue craft paper**, and write *The World of Words* across the top. Invite children to **glue** the printed words on the "globe." Read aloud some of the words.

3 Invite volunteers to dictate sentences for you to write on a piece of **chart paper**. Ask children *Why do we write the words on the paper?*

4 Invite children to write a message to a friend in class. Remind children that they will use their **pencils** to write on **paper** the words that will convey their message. Encourage children to write their message as best they can. Any form of writing, including invented spellings and strings of letters, symbols, or numbers, displays their emerging knowledge that print conveys meaning.

5 Ask families to write a short letter to their children, which they should give you in a sealed envelope. Deliver the **letters** to the children, and read each one aloud. Remind children that their families used print to tell them their messages.

Name ______________________ Date ______________

Print Conveys Meaning

Write a note to say whether or not you will go to the party.

Identifying Uppercase and Lowercase Letters

The reader will recognize the difference between uppercase and lowercase letters.

Use this activity to show children that words and print are made up of uppercase and lowercase letters. Show children individual letters in different kinds of printed materials. Tell children there are two kinds of letters they will need to know in order to read. Explain that the big letters are *uppercase letters* and the small letters are *lowercase letters*.

Display uppercase and lowercase alphabet cards. Use a pointer to point to a letter, and ask individual children to name its case and its name. For example, point to *R*, and prompt a child to say *Uppercase r*. Invite volunteers to use the pointer to point out other letters for their classmates to identify.

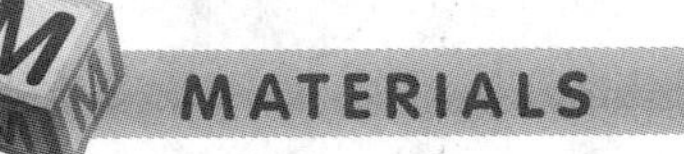

- printed materials (e.g., picture books, magazines, pamphlets)
- alphabet cards (uppercase and lowercase)
- pointer (see page 6)

Write the uppercase and lowercase versions of each letter of the alphabet on separate index cards. Place the uppercase letters in the top rows of the pocket chart. Place the lowercase letters in the bottom rows. Invite children to match the lowercase and uppercase letters. Give each child an Uppercase- and Lowercase-Letter Search reproducible. Read aloud the directions on the paper, and tell children to follow the directions.

Print each child's name on a separate index card. Write the first letter of each name in red and the remaining letters in green. Place each card in a pocket of the chart. Ask children why the first letter is printed in red (i.e., it is an uppercase letter, and all names begin with an uppercase letter). Ask children why the remaining letters are printed in a different color (i.e., they are the lowercase letters). Invite children to locate their name in the pocket chart.

MATERIALS

- Uppercase- and Lowercase-Letter Search reproducible (page 23)
- index cards
- pocket chart
- markers (red and green)

1 Invite children to use **art supplies (e.g., paint, play dough, yarn, and Wikki Stix)** to form uppercase and lowercase letters.

2 Write uppercase and lowercase letters on separate **index cards**, and place them at a learning center. Invite children to separate the cards into uppercase and lowercase piles.

3 Sing the alphabet song daily, and point to the corresponding uppercase **alphabet cards** as you sing. Repeat with the lowercase alphabet cards.

4 Invite children to use **magnifying glasses or plastic sunglasses** with the lenses removed to go on a "letter hunt" around the room. Challenge children to find a variety of lowercase and uppercase letters.

5 Place **crayons**, **markers**, **pencils**, and **paper** of various colors, sizes, and shapes at a learning center where the alphabet is displayed. Invite children to use the writing supplies to write the uppercase and lowercase letters of the alphabet.

Name ________________________ Date ____________

Uppercase- and Lowercase-Letter Search

Circle the uppercase letters in red.
Circle the lowercase letters in green.

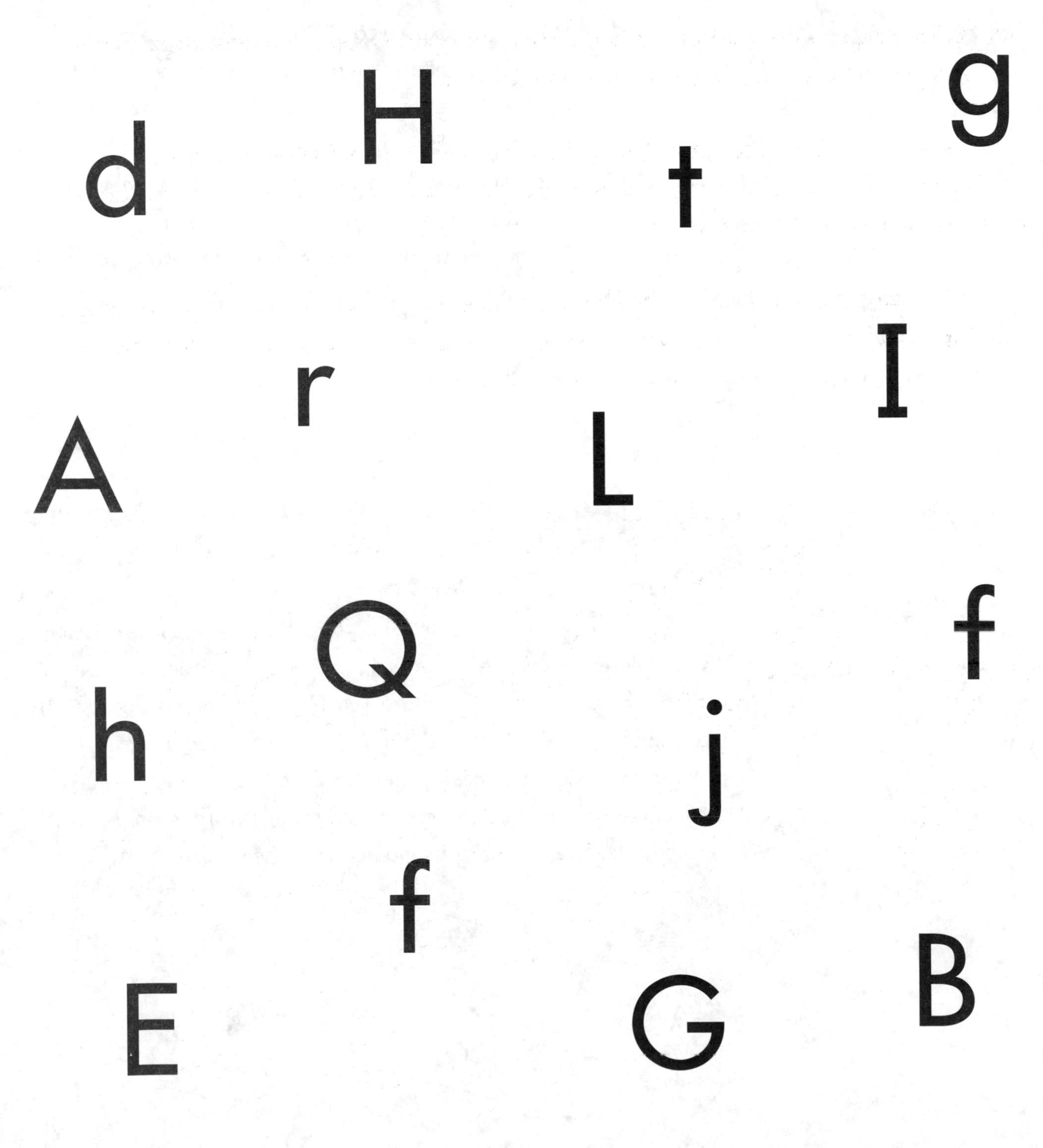

Combining Letters Makes Words

The reader will understand that words are made up of individual letters.

MATERIALS

- magnetic letters/ magnetic board

Explain to children that there are 26 different letters of the alphabet, and that letters are put together to make words. Place three magnetic letters on a board to make a CVC (consonant-vowel-consonant) word, such as *cat* or *dog*. As you place each letter on the board, remind children that words are made up of individual letters. Slowly separate the letters to show children that the word can be divided into individual letters.

MATERIALS

- Letters Make Words reproducibles (pages 26–27)
- envelopes
- crayons
- scissors

Write *you*, *can*, *see*, *the*, *big*, and *dog* on six separate envelopes. Make a set for each child. Give each child a set of envelopes and a set of Letters Make Words reproducibles. Invite children to color each letter in each word a different color. Tell children to cut out their first word, *you*. Have children cut apart each letter in the word and place it in the envelope marked "you." Invite children to repeat with *the*, *big*, and *dog*. Encourage children to take their envelopes home for extra practice making words from letters. Challenge children to make a sentence with their words.

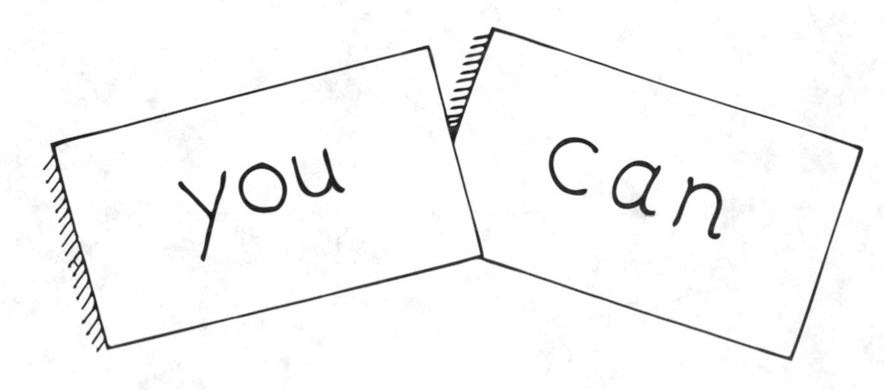

1 Sing the alphabet song daily, and point to the corresponding **alphabet cards** as you sing. Remind children that *l*, *m*, *n*, and *o* are separate letters. Invite volunteers to point to the letters as the class sings.

2 Give children **alphabet soup** to eat, and ask them to name the individual letters in their soup.

3 Give children dry **alphabet cereal** to eat, and have them write each letter before they eat it.

4 Write children's names on separate **index cards**. Show children how to take two index cards and cover the first and last parts of their name to reveal a middle letter, and ask them to name it. Invite children to move their index card "frame" to reveal other individual letters, and have children name the letters.

5 Write each child's name on a separate index card, and place the cards in the pockets of a **pocket chart**. Point to one card, and invite children to help you count the number of letters in the name. Repeat with other name cards.

6 Write each child's name on a separate index card, and give each child his or her name card. Tell children to use a **marker** to circle or underline each letter in their name.

Letters Make Words

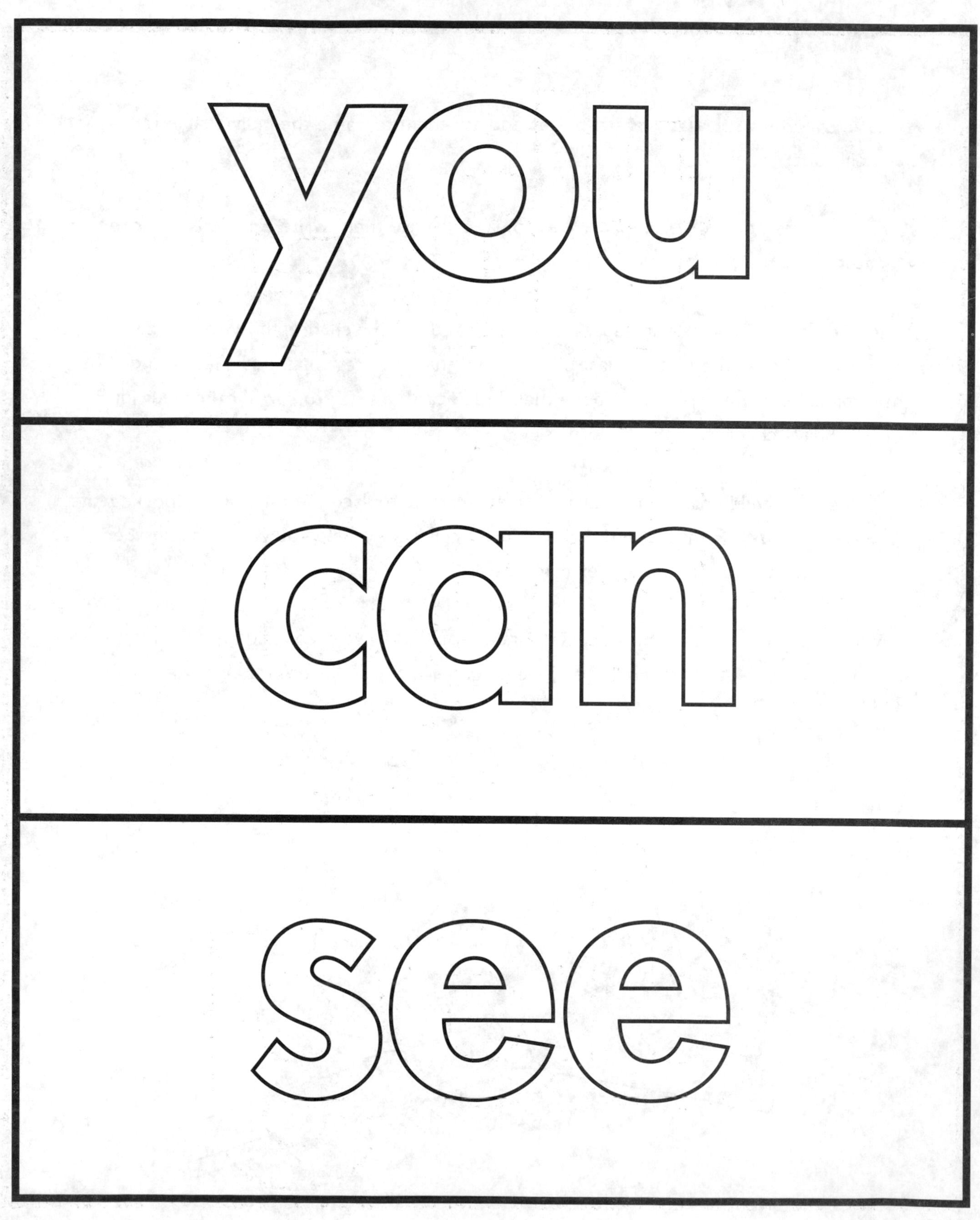

Letters Make Words

Working with Words

The reader will recognize words.

MATERIALS

- chart paper
- pointer (see page 6)
- marker
- sentence strip
- scissors
- pocket chart

Explain to children that the words we say when we read a story are the same words that are printed on the page. Write a short story or poem on chart paper, and display it. Read the text aloud. Use the star pointer to emphasize that the words are separated by spaces. Use a marker to circle individual words in a few lines of text. Count the words as you circle them. Write one of the sentences from the text on a sentence strip. Cut apart each word of the sentence. Explain to children that you knew where to cut because there was a space between each word. Give volunteers separate words. Ask these children to place their cards in a pocket chart in the order that the words appear on the chart paper.

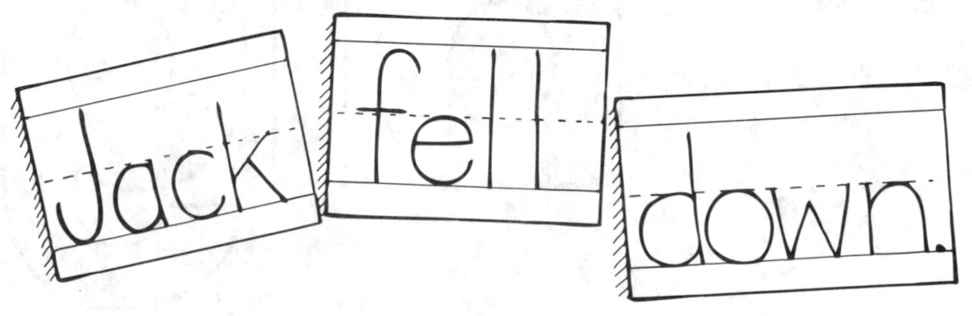

- Working with Words reproducibles (pages 30–31)
- sentence strip
- pocket chart
- index cards
- marker

On a sentence strip, write *I am a big kid.* Then place it in the pocket of a chart. Show children how to take two index cards to frame an individual word. Give a volunteer two index cards, and ask him or her to frame a word in the sentence. Give other children an opportunity to frame particular words. For example, say *Frame the word that starts with* ***k*** or *Frame the word with two letters.* After children have practiced framing the words of the sentence, circle each word with a marker. Ask children to count the words as you circle them. Give each child a set of the Working with Words reproducibles. Read aloud the directions on the paper, and tell children to follow the directions.

Reinforcing THE Concept

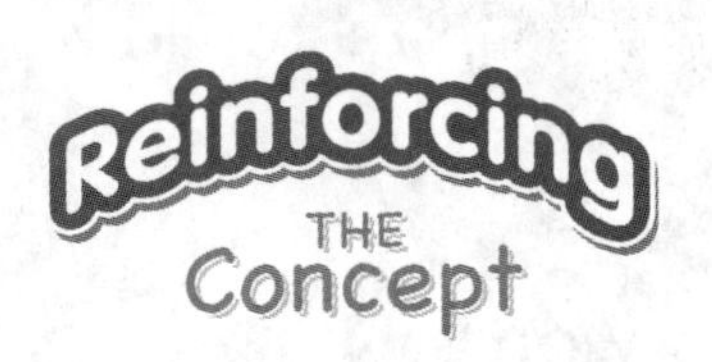

1 Invite children to help you write a story. As you write their ideas on a piece of **chart paper**, explain that you are leaving a space between each word they say.

2 Invite children to use **scissors** to cut out words from a **magazine**, and have them **glue** the words in a line on a **sentence strip**. Remind children to leave spaces between their words. Read aloud children's silly sentences.

3 Write the following sentences on a **board** or chart paper:

I'm hot.
Are you hot?
I hope you're not.
I don't like being hot!

4 Ask a volunteer to use the star **pointer (see page 6)** to point to the sentence with four words. Ask other volunteers to point to the sentences with two, three, and five words.

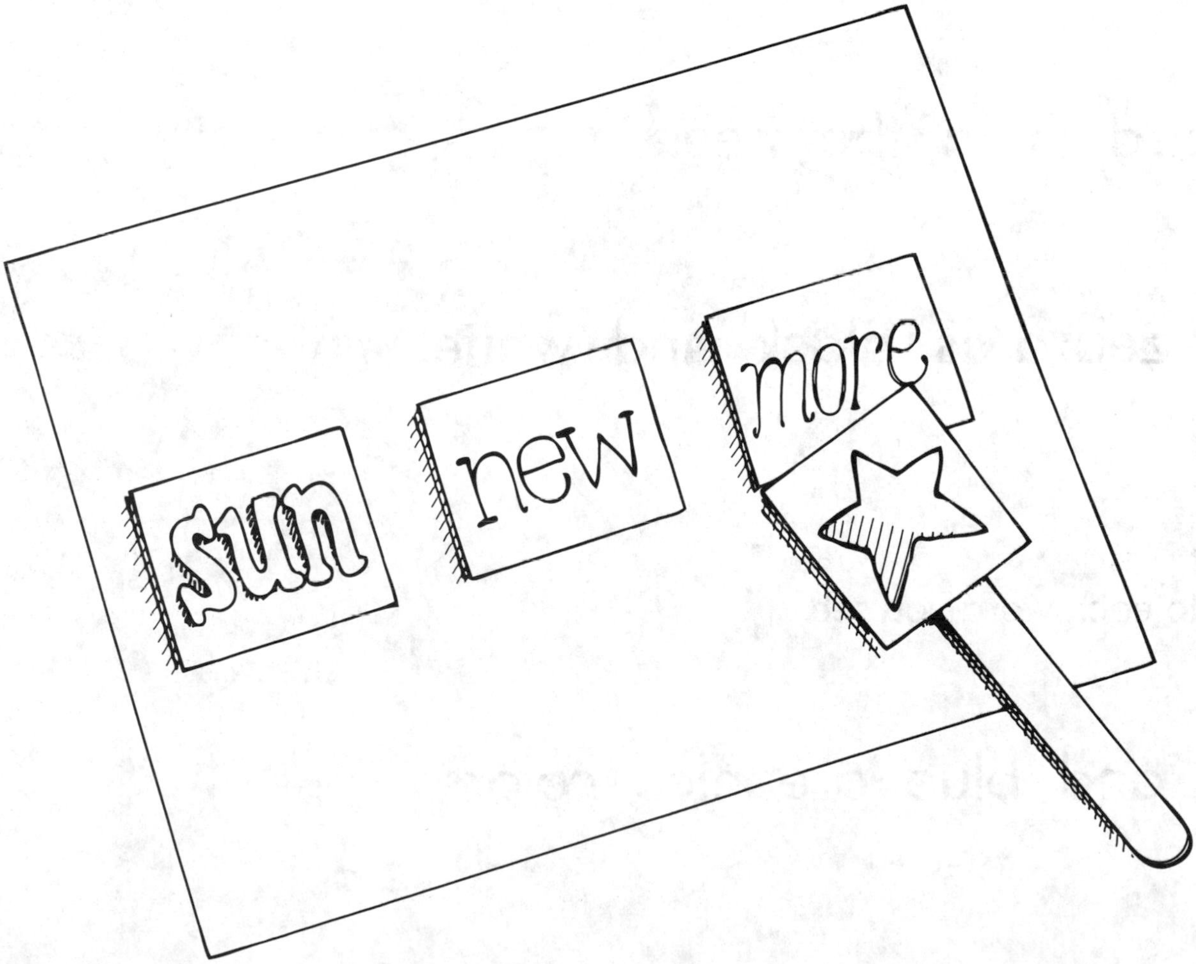

Name ______________________________ Date ________________

Working with Words

Count the words in each sentence. Circle the number of words.

I like you.	1	2	3	4	5
You are my friend.	1	2	3	4	5

Circle each word in each sentence.

A bird is in the tree.

The zebra is black and white.

Point to each word you see.

Red and blue are nice colors.

Name ______________________ Date ______________

Working with Words

Cut out the words. Read the words. Arrange the words to make a sentence.

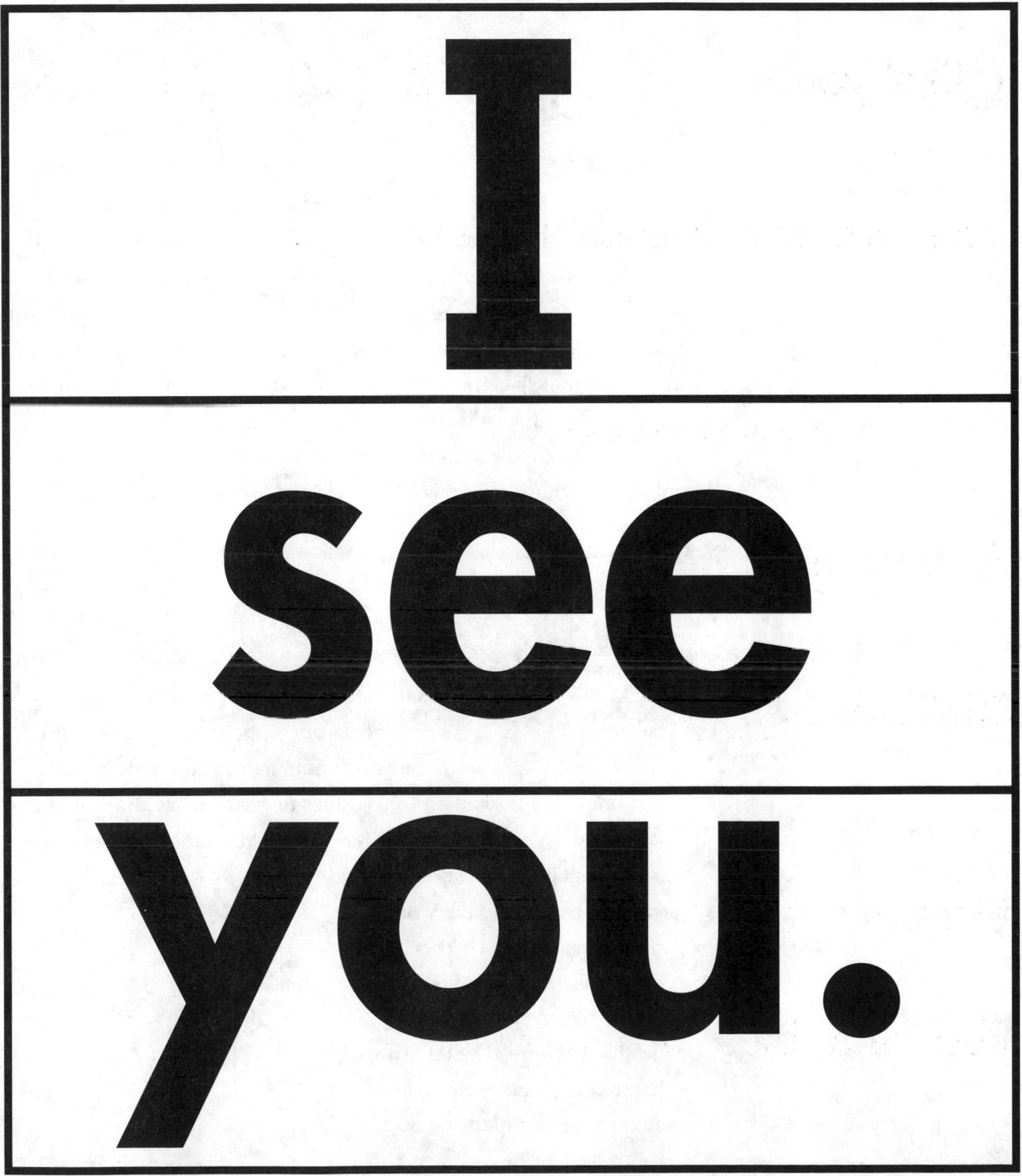

Recognizing First and Last

The reader will demonstrate an understanding of first and last.

MATERIALS

- big book
- pointer (see page 6)

Display a big book. Show children the first page of the book, and use a pointer to point to the first word. Remind children that the first word on the first page is where we begin to read. Page through the book to the last page, and identify it as such. Return to the first page, circle the first word with your finger, and begin reading. Continue reading the selection until you come to the last word on the first page. Circle the last word on the page with your finger, and tell children that the last word on a page is a clue that either it is time to turn the page or the story is over. Turn the page, and continue reading to the end of the book. Invite volunteers to use their finger to circle the first and last words on each page of the book.

MATERIALS

- First and Last reproducibles (pages 34–35)
- sentence strips
- pocket chart
- index cards

Write three sentences from a story on separate sentence strips, and place them in a pocket of a pocket chart. Use index cards to frame individual words in the sentences. Invite children to use their finger to circle the first and last words in each sentence. Give each child a set of First and Last reproducibles. Tell children you will read aloud the words on the paper. Ask children to place a finger on the first word. Invite children to point to the words as you read aloud "The Itsy-Bitsy Spider." Help children answer the questions on both reproducibles.

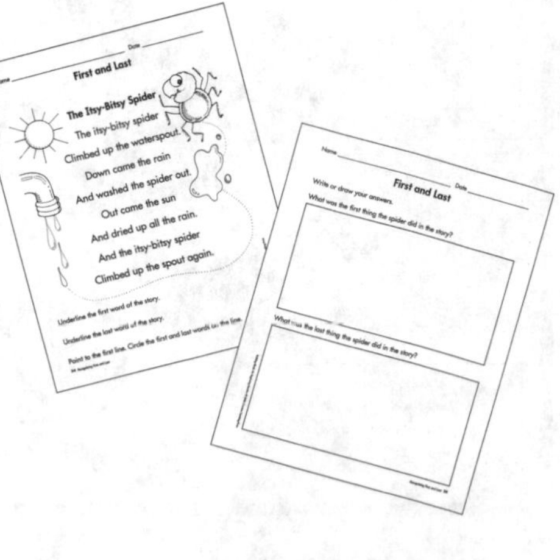

Name Date

First and Last

The Itsy-Bitsy Spider

The itsy-bitsy spider
Climbed up the waterspout.
Down came the rain
And washed the spider out.
Out came the sun
And dried up all the rain.
And the itsy-bitsy spider
Climbed up the spout again.

Underline the first word of the story.

Underline the last word of the story.

Point to the first line. Circle the first and last words on the line.

Name Date

First and Last

Write or draw your answers.

What was the first thing the spider did in the story?

What was the last thing the spider did in the story?

1 Write children's first names on separate **index cards**. Place the cards on a ledge or in the pockets of a **pocket chart**. Invite a child to say his or her first name. Ask the same child to locate his or her name card and read it. Give the child a **marker**, and ask the child to write his or her name on a piece of **chart paper**. Invite another child to repeat the activity until each child has had a turn.

2 Write each child's last name on an index card, and repeat the activity above.

3 Invite the children to stand in a line. Ask children to name who is first and last in line. Rearrange the children, and ask children to name who is now first and last in line.

4 Discuss with children the first thing they do in the morning and the last thing they do before they go to bed at night.

5 Perform a sequence of three movements, such as jump, clap, snap. Ask children to imitate the first movement you did. Ask children to imitate the last movement you did. Invite volunteers to perform a sequence of three movements, and invite children to imitate the first and last actions.

Name ______________________________ Date ____________________

First and Last

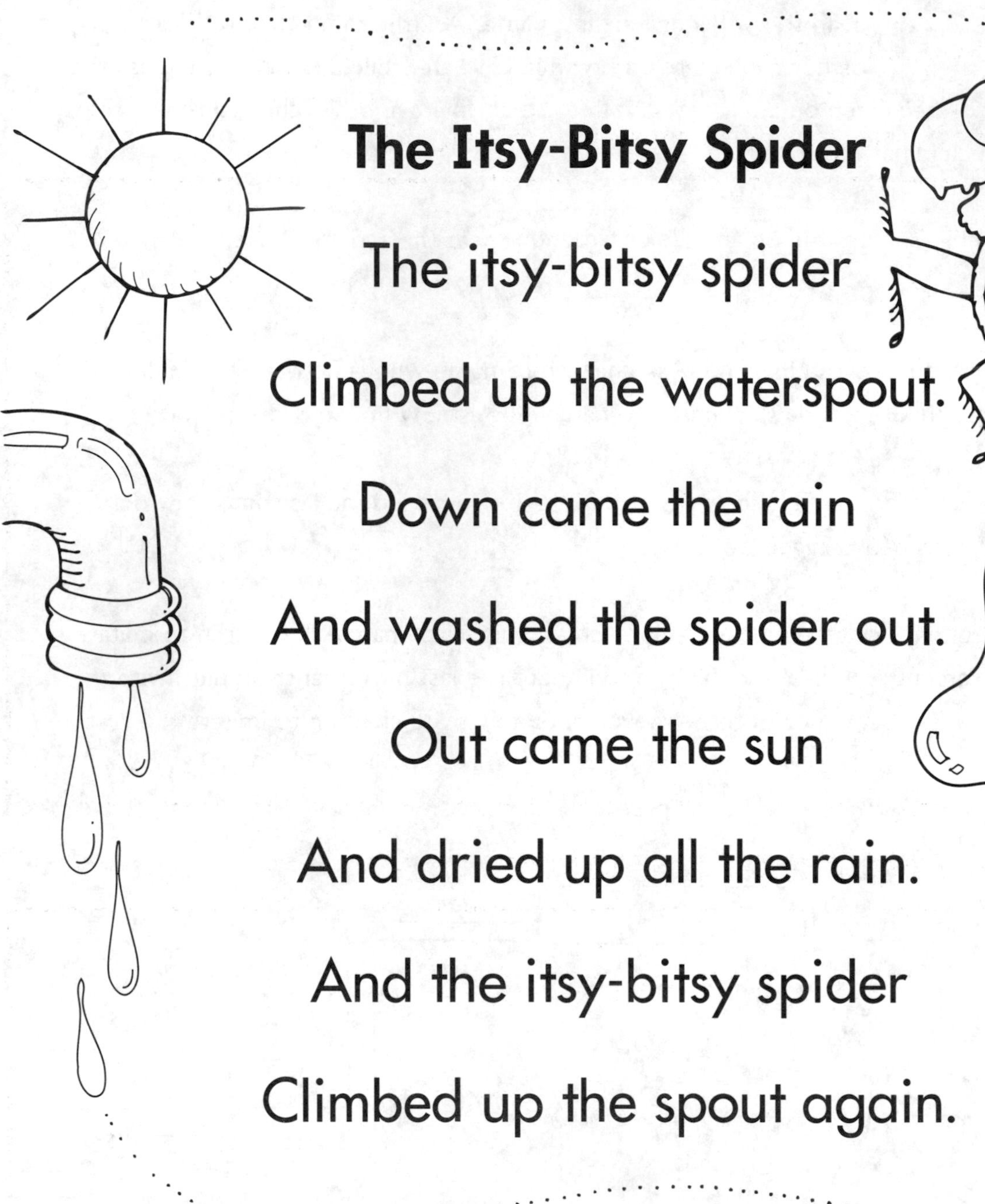

The Itsy-Bitsy Spider

The itsy-bitsy spider
Climbed up the waterspout.
Down came the rain
And washed the spider out.
Out came the sun
And dried up all the rain.
And the itsy-bitsy spider
Climbed up the spout again.

Underline the first word of the story.

Underline the last word of the story.

Point to the first line. Circle the first and last words on the line.

Name ______________________________ Date ____________________

First and Last

Write or draw your answers.

What was the first thing the spider did in the story?

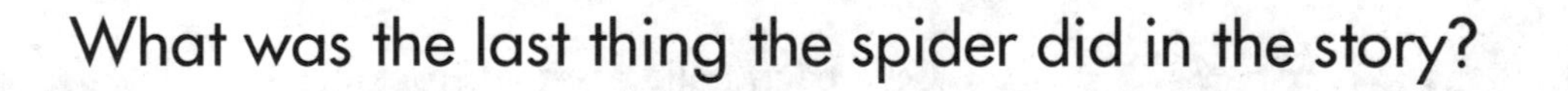
What was the last thing the spider did in the story?

Tracking

The reader will correlate the number of spoken words with the number of printed words on a page.

MATERIALS

- big book
- pointer (see page 6)
- sentence strip
- pocket chart

Display a big book. Slowly read the story. Use the star pointer to point to each word you read. Reread the story. Invite children to clap each time you point to a word. Write a sentence from the story on a sentence strip, and place it in a pocket of the pocket chart. Slowly read aloud the sentence. Tell children you will read the sentence again, and ask them to count the number of words you say. Point to the words in the sentence on the strip. Ask children to count the number of words with you. Prompt children to say that the number of words they heard matches the number of words they see on the sentence strip. Invite volunteers to use the pointer to help them read the sentence. Encourage children to point to one word on the strip for each word they say.

MATERIALS

- Tracking reproducibles (pages 38–39)
- crayons
- scissors

Give each child a set of Tracking reproducibles. Invite children to color and cut out the train on the first page. Tell children to point to the first sentence on the next page. Have children place their train cutout under the first word in the sentence. Slowly read aloud the first sentence. Have children slide their train below each word you read. Ask children to count how many times they moved their train. Ask children to count the number of words in the sentence. Prompt children to say that the number of times the train moved (including the first time they placed it on the track) is the same as the number of words in the sentence. Repeat with the remaining sentence.

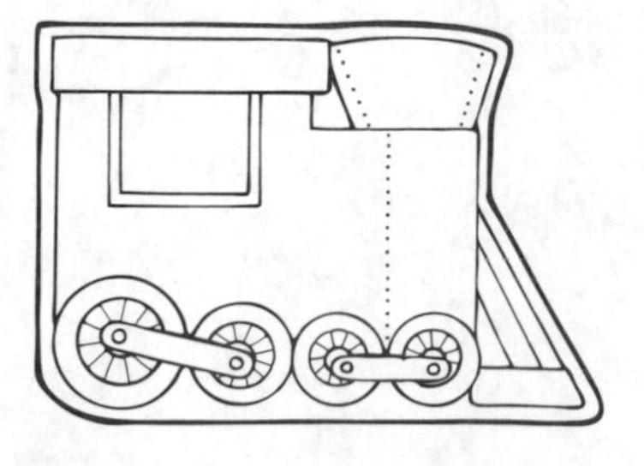

1 Write sentences on **sentence strips**, and place them in the pocket of a **pocket chart**. Invite children to stand. Use the star **pointer (see page 6)** to point to each word in each sentence as you read it. Ask children to hop in place every time they hear a word.

2 Choose a story that is familiar to the children, choose a sentence with three to five words from the story, and write the words on a sentence strip. Repeat with two more sentences from the story. Place the sentence strips in the pocket of a pocket chart. Give each child five **linking cubes**. Tell children to snap together one cube for each word they hear. Read the first sentence slowly, and prompt children to make a tower with the same number of cubes as words in the sentence.

3 Read with each child individually. Give a child a **book** and a pointer (see page 6). Help the child use the pointer to point to each word you read together.

Name ______________________________ Date ________________

Tracking

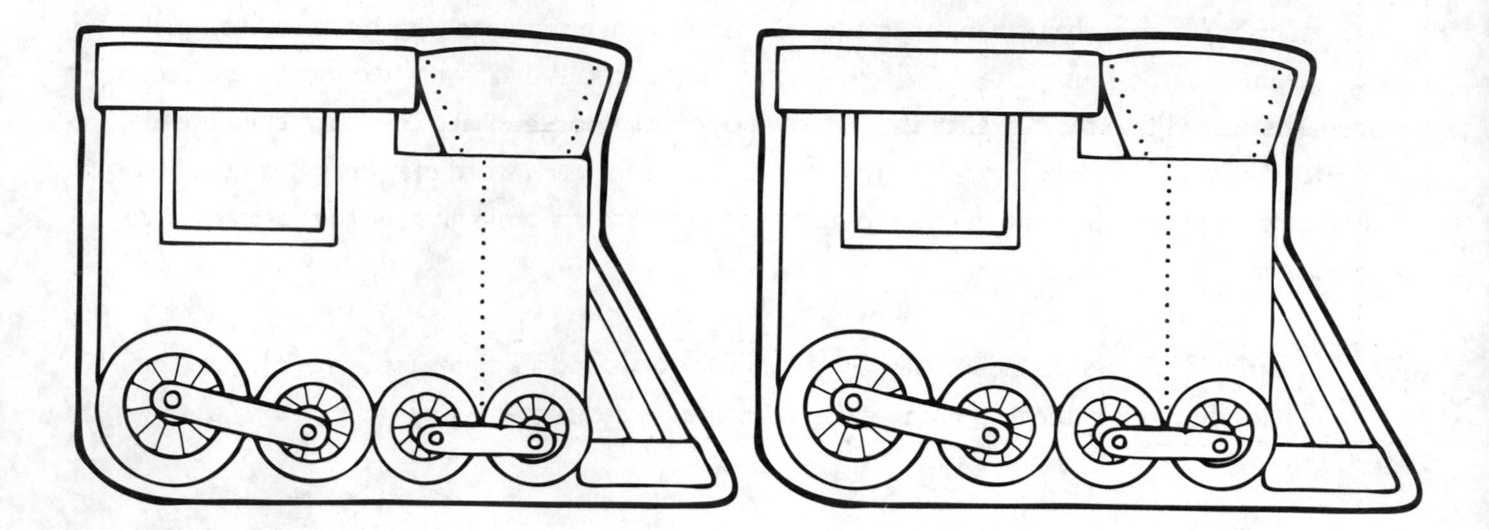

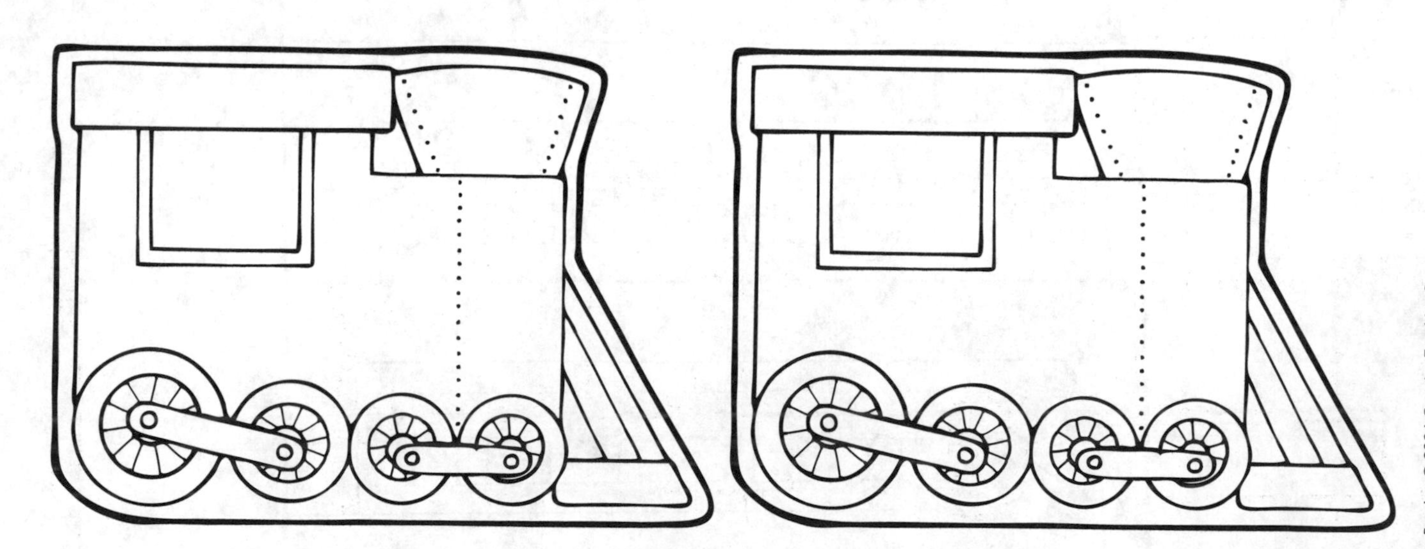

Name ______________________ Date ______________

Tracking

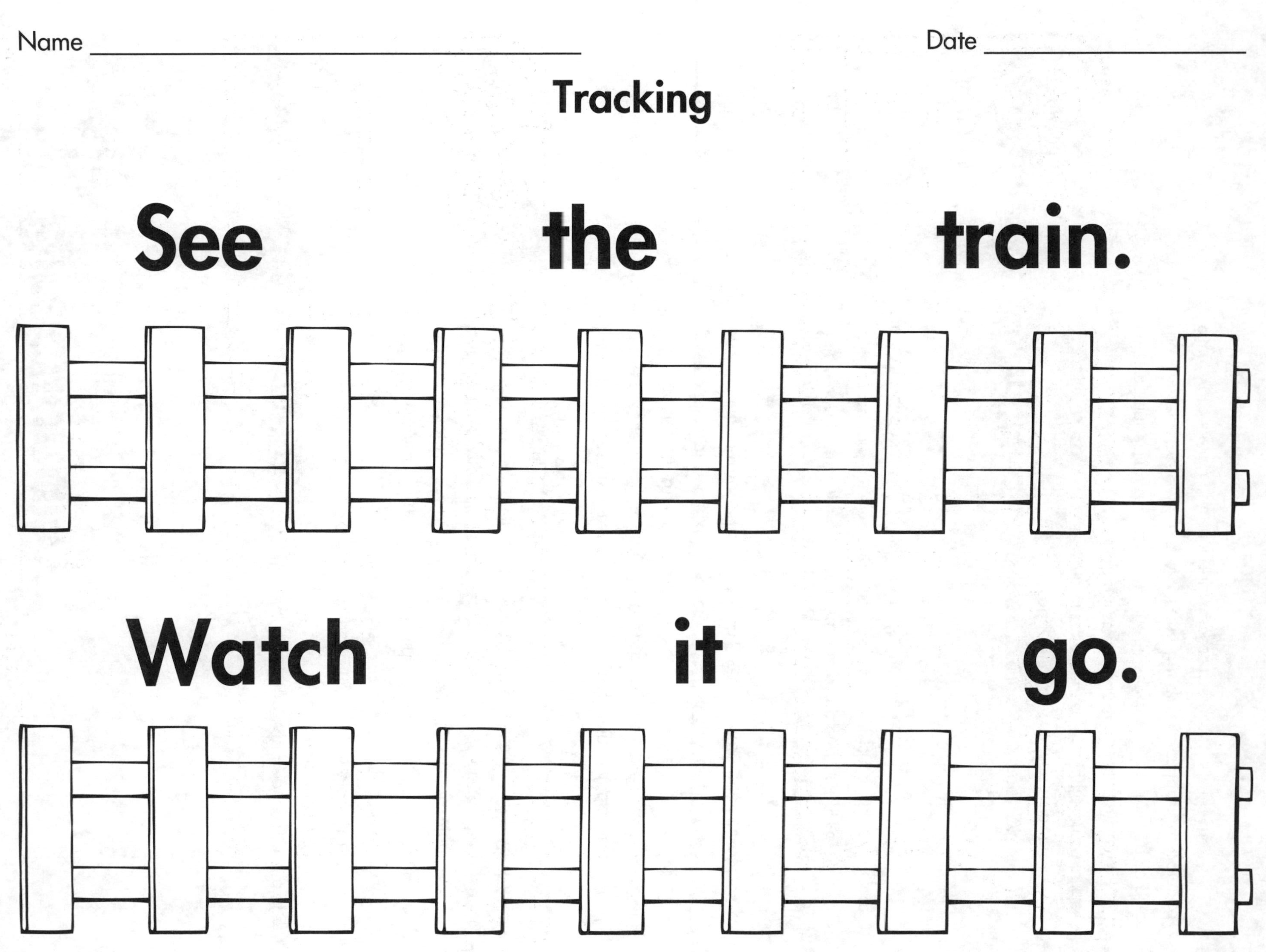

Directionality

The reader will demonstrate how to read text from left to right.

MATERIALS

- big book
- pointers (see page 6)
- sticky note

Display a big book, and open it to the first page of text. Use the pointer with the arrow pointing left to indicate the first word. Use the pointers with the arrows pointing right and down to show children how we read from left to right and from the top to the bottom of a page. Give a volunteer a sticky note, and tell him or her to affix it to the place where we begin reading. Ask children to point in the direction in which we will continue reading.

Place the broom pointer on the first word again. Point to each word in the text as you read the first page. Exaggerate the action of moving the pointer from the end of one line of text to the beginning of the next line of text. Explain to children that this is called *sweeping*. Invite children to use the pointer to "sweep" from one line of text to the next.

Ask children what we do when we get to the end of a page. Invite a child to be the "page turner." Ask the remaining children to indicate the direction in which the page must be turned.

MATERIALS

- Directionality reproducible (page 42)

Give each child a Directionality reproducible. Tell children to point to the first sentence. Ask children to circle the first word in the sentence. Have children underline the last word in the sentence. Tell children to place their finger on the word they circled. Encourage children to point to each word as you read it aloud. Repeat the process with the remaining sentences.

1 Invite children to play a game of Simon Says. Give children directions that involve left and right. For example, say *Simon Says touch your left ear* or *Simon Says wave your right hand.*

2 Write the letters of the alphabet on separate **index cards**, and place them at a learning center with a **pocket chart**. Place the *A* card in the top left pocket. Invite children to arrange the remaining cards in alphabetical order from left to right.

3 Place a set of **magnetic shapes** and a **magnetic board** at a learning center. Invite children to make pattern "sentences" with the shapes. Remind children to begin at the left side of the board and move to the right.

Name ______________________________ Date ____________________

Directionality

Circle the first word in each sentence.
Underline the last word in each sentence

A bird flew in the sky.

The brown dog runs fast.

The fish swims in the lake.

Sentences

The reader will understand the function of punctuation.

Tell children that good readers change their voice when they read to help the listener understand what is happening in a story. Copy and cut apart a set of Punctuation Cards. Raise the card with the period on it. Tell children that a period appears at the end of a sentence. Explain that a period shows the reader when to stop to take a breath. Raise the card with the question mark on it. Tell children that this symbol means the character is asking a question. Explain to children that a question is a special kind of sentence that requires an answer. Raise the card with the exclamation point on it. Tell children that this symbol tells the reader to read the sentence with feeling. Explain that the exclamation point helps the reader know whether the character feels happy, excited, angry, or scared.

- Punctuation Cards (page 45)
- scissors
- big book

Make a set of Punctuation Cards, and give each child one card. Use sticky notes to cover the punctuation on a page of the big book. Tell children that you will read each sentence, and ask them to listen to your voice to determine which punctuation belongs at the end of it. Invite children to raise the correct card after you read each sentence. Remove the sticky note after children raise their cards to help them determine whether or not they were correct.

MATERIALS

- Punctuation Cards (page 45)
- sticky notes
- big book

1 Give children **plastic sunglasses** with the lenses removed, and invite them to "read the room." Encourage children to use their glasses to help them see print in the classroom.

2 Give children photocopied pages of print, and invite them to use **markers** to circle, underline, or highlight the punctuation they see.

3 Invite children to work with a partner. Give each pair of children a set of **Punctuation Cards (page 45)**. Prompt one child in each pair to ask a question. For example, say *What do you ask your mom or dad when you can't find your shoes?* Invite the other child to display the Punctuation Card that appropriately marks what the partner just said. Invite children to take turns making statements, asking questions, making exclamations, and displaying Punctuation Cards.

Name ______________________ Date ______________

Punctuation Cards

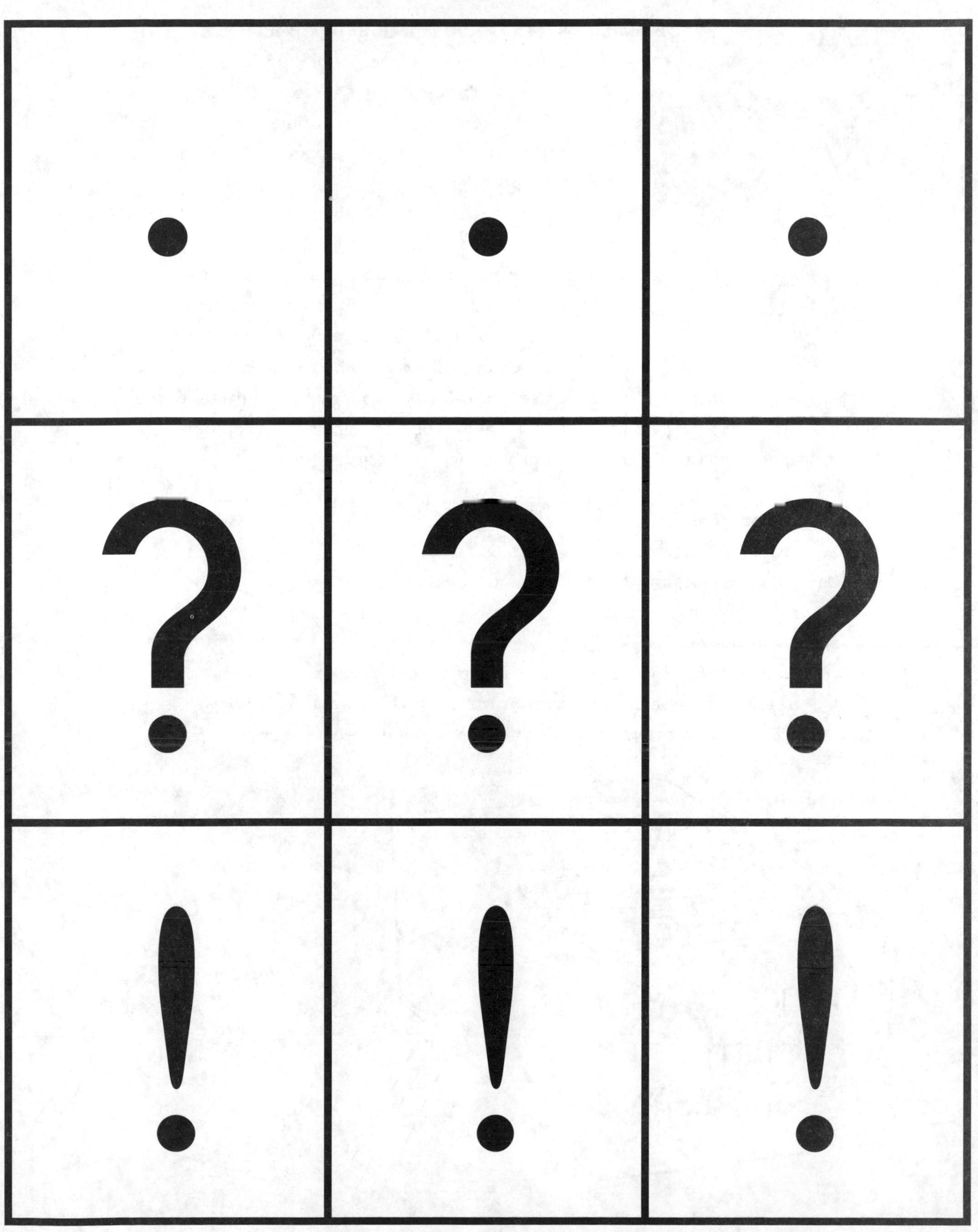

Assessment

How to Assess Understanding of Concepts of Print

Make four copies of the Concepts of Print Assessment Tool reproducibles (pages 47–48) for each child. Use the Assessment Tool at four different times over the school year to monitor children's developing understanding of the concepts of print.

Use a color code to identify each child's performance level during each assessment. For example, use a yellow marker to highlight the names of children who demonstrate an understanding of the concepts of print, use a blue marker to highlight the names of the children who are close to demonstrating an understanding of the concepts of print, and use a green marker to highlight the names of the children who are struggling. This system will allow you to group children appropriately for instruction and easily identify children who need extra attention.

Assessment Tips

- Assess each child individually.
- Administer the assessment in a quiet location without interruption.
- Gather the following materials for use in the assessment: beginning reading books, a pointer, and index cards.
- When a child struggles to demonstrate a skill, move on to the next concept. When a child struggles with several skills, postpone the assessment. Give the child opportunities to practice concepts before attempting the assessment procedure again.

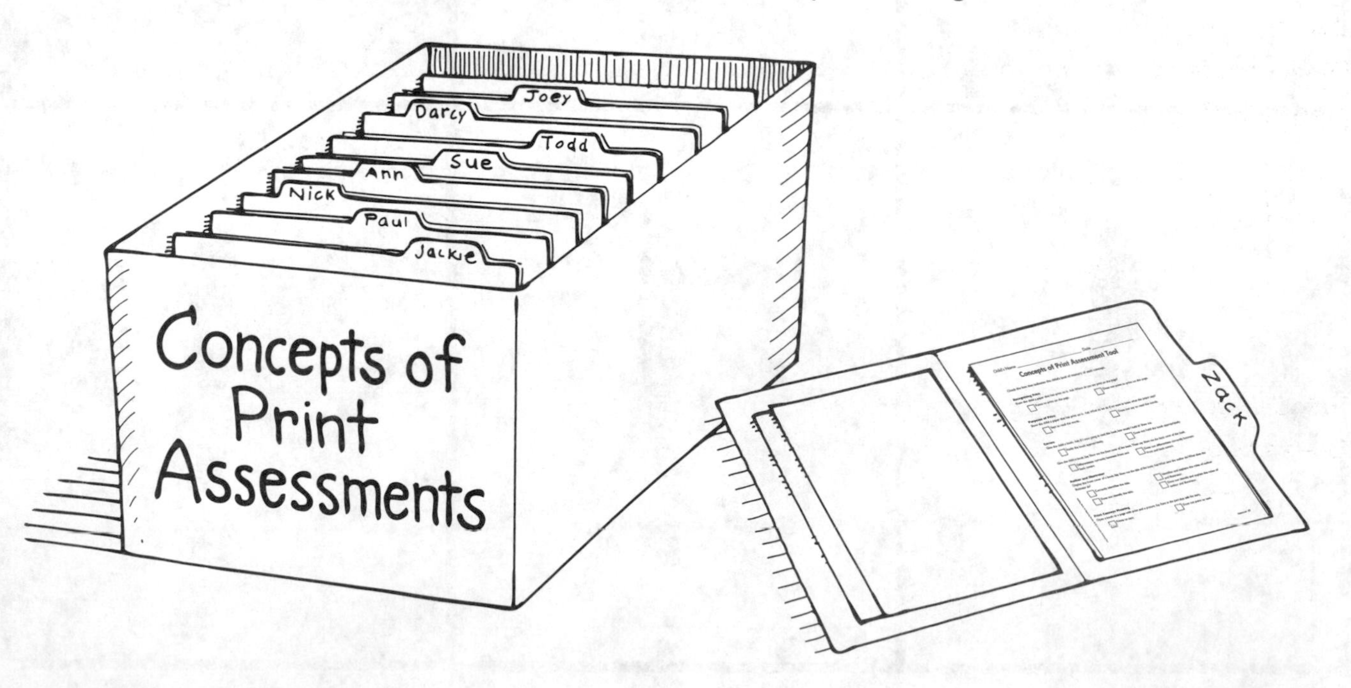

Child's Name ______________________________ Date ____________________

Concepts of Print Assessment Tool

Check the box that indicates the child's level of mastery of each concept.

Recognizing Print

Show the child a paper that has print on it. Ask *Where do you see print on this page?*

☐ Points to print on the page. ☐ Does not point to print on the page.

Purposes of Print

Show the child a paper that has print on it. Ask *What do we do if we want to know what this paper says?*

☐ Says to read the words. ☐ Does not say to read the words.

Covers

Give the child a book. Ask *If I were going to read this book, how would I hold it? Show me.*

☐ Holds the book appropriately. ☐ Does not hold the book appropriately.

Give the child a book. Say *Show me the front cover of the book.* Then say *Show me the back cover of the book.*

☐ Differentiates correctly between front and back covers. ☐ Does not differentiate correctly between front and back covers.

Author and Illustrator

Display the front cover of a book. Say *Show me the title of the book.* Ask *What does the author do? What does the illustrator do?*

☐ Correctly identifies the title. ☐ Identifies and explains the roles of author and illustrator.

☐ Does not identify the title. ☐ Does not identify and explain the roles of author and illustrator.

Print Conveys Meaning

Open a book to a page with print and a picture. Say *Point to the part that tells the story.*

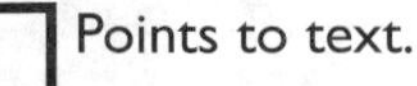

☐ Points to text. ☐ Does not point to text.

Identifying Uppercase and Lowercase Letters

Point to print in a book. Say *Point to an uppercase letter. Name the letter. Point to a lowercase letter. Name the letter.*

 Recognizes and identifies uppercase and lowercase letters.

Does not recognize and identify uppercase and lowercase letters.

Combining Letters Makes Words

Display a page of print. Say *Point to a word. What is this word made of?*

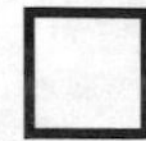 Understands that letters make words.

Does not understand that letters make words.

Working with Words

Give the child two index cards, and display a page of print. Say *Use these cards to show me only one word on this page.*

 Identifies individual words.

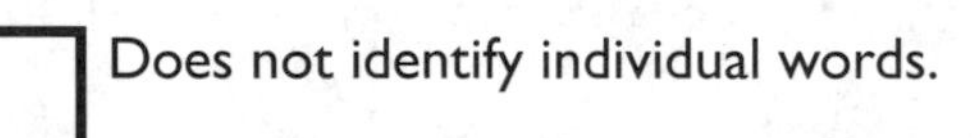 Does not identify individual words.

Recognizing First and Last

Give the child a book. Say *Turn to the first page in this book. Turn to the last page in this book.* Use index cards to frame one sentence on a page of print. Say *Point to the first and last words in this sentence.* Frame one word. Say *Tell me the first and last letters in this word.* Say *Use your finger to circle the first word on this page. Use your finger to circle the last word on the page.*

 Understands first and last.

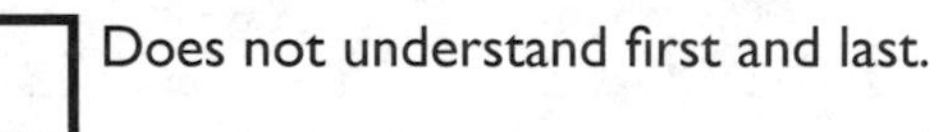 Does not understand first and last.

Tracking

Use index cards to frame one sentence on a page of print. Say *I am going to read this sentence. Point to each word I read.*

 Understands one-to-one correspondence.

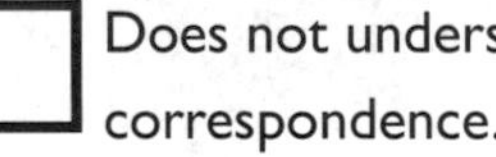 Does not understand one-to-one correspondence.

Directionality

Display a page with several lines of print. Say *Show me where to begin reading. Show me which way should I go after that. Show me what to do after I finish reading a line. Show me what to do after I read a page.*

 Understands directionality.

 Does not understand directionality.

Sentences

Display a page of a book that features a period, a question mark, and an exclamation point. Point to each punctuation mark separately, and ask *What is this called?*

 Recognizes all punctuation marks.

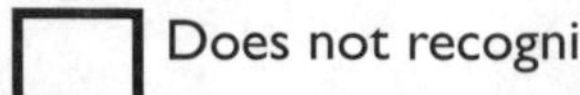 Does not recognize all punctuation marks.